Other Books by Kassandra Lamb

The Kate Huntington Mysteries
Psychotherapist Kate Huntington helps others cope with trauma, but she has led a charmed life...until a killer rips it apart. (10 novels) Plus 4 **Kate on Vacation** novellas.

~

The Marcia Banks and Buddy Cozy Mysteries
Marcia Banks trains service dogs for veterans, and solves crimes on the side, with the help of her Black Lab, Buddy. (13 novels/novellas)

~

The C.o.P. on the Scene Mysteries
Eight days into her new job as Chief of Police in a small Florida city, Judith Anderson finds herself one step behind a serial killer. (spinoff from the Kate Huntington series; 3 stories–more to come)

~

The Unintended Consequences Trilogy
writing as Jessica Dale ~ A sweet romance combined with three chilling mysteries, and a couple of ghosts. (3 stories)

The TWELVE HEISTS of CHRISTMAS

A C.o.P. on the Scene Short Mystery

Kassandra Lamb

a misterio press publication

CHAPTER ONE

December 21ˢᵗ ~ 8:00 a.m.

The winter solstice—the shortest day of the year. *Ha!* That had *not* been my experience so far this morning.

As usual, I'd risen at five-thirty and gone for a two-mile run along the riverwalk. It was blissfully deserted at that hour, only the wreaths adorning the lamp posts keeping me company. I'd scowled at them. This is not my favorite time of year.

By six-forty, I was showered and dressed in my standard work attire, black pantsuit and white shirt, and was heading for the municipal building, home of my police department as well as the city government's offices.

During the short drive, my mind—like one's tongue poking at a sore tooth—stubbornly returned to yesterday's discussion with an unhappy shop owner.

"What can I say, Chief?" The middle-aged, paunchy guy had a faint Jersey accent. "A fat dude in a Santa mask comes in, all ho, ho, ho. The customers are smiling, and the next thing I know the guy's smashing up my display cases and grabbing stuff."

I'd nodded, encouraging him to keep talking.

"I mean, I got a gun, all legal and such, but the customers are now staring. Whadaya gonna do? Am I gonna shoot Santa?" His voice had gone up several notches in pitch as he'd shrugged.

I'd glanced at my assistant, Officer Gloria Barnes—a rookie, but I swear her soul is older than mine. Her expression neutral, she'd given a slight shake of her head. I wasn't sure what that meant. Was she for or against shooting Santa?

I'd reassured the shop owner that he'd done the right thing. Best not to open fire on St. Nick, especially with a store full of customers.

That was the sixth such discussion I'd had in the last week.

Once in my office on the third floor of the municipal building—not so affectionately called 3MB by my officers—I'd poured my first mug of liquid caffeine and booted up my computer.

The morning reports contained two more smash-and-grab robberies by someone in a Santa mask—a gift shop and an electronics store. They'd happened at seven-ten and eight-fifteen the previous evening.

Four strikes yesterday. This guy was getting bolder. If it was a guy.

We had practically no description—at least not a consistent one. Some witnesses had said the perp was tall and thin, others that he was medium height and thin, and still others that he was medium height and heavy.

Or maybe he was a she?

I used the pronoun "he" only because thinking "he or she" took too damn long. The only consistencies were that he wore a plastic Santa mask—with rosy cheeks, a jolly smile, and a fake beard attached—plus a hoodie and gloves. Witnesses even disagreed about the color of the hoodie. Was it black, dark gray or navy?

Race varied as well, some witnesses saying he was white, some black, and a couple swearing he was Hispanic. My guess was these were all assumptions, since every part of his body was covered with clothing or the mask and beard.

Even the targeted shops were not consistent. Some were gift shops that, like the one last night, carried rather cheap merchandise, and some were toy stores. The stolen merchandise amounted to a few hundred dollars, if that.

But about half the targets were jewelry, electronics, or high-end gift shops. The hauls from those heists were much more valuable.

Another robbery call came in while I was reviewing the reports, this time a toy store, on the east side of town. It had just opened, earlier than usual because it was only four days until Christmas, and the first person through the door had been Hoodie Santa—as the press had dubbed him. He'd filled his pockets with video games, then took off.

My private line rang ten minutes later. It was the mayor of our fair city of Starling, Florida, population approximately eleven-thousand souls. But we bordered the much larger and more crime-ridden city of Jacksonville.

After the requisite ass-chewing from the mayor, the next call was tame by comparison. The chair of the city council was somewhat calmer but equally concerned about the crime wave. "Chief, we just can't have this. People are telling me that they're driving to Jacksonville to finish their Christmas shopping. They actually feel safer there, in *Jacksonville!*" His voice went up to a borderline screech.

"I understand your concern, Councilman," I said in my best soothing voice. "I've doubled patrols in the shopping districts."

But this guy is fast, I added in my head. Even when the shopkeeper triggered a silent alarm while the perp was still on the premises, he was long gone by the time our officers arrived.

"I can call an emergency council meeting," the councilman said. "Try to get you some more resources."

I ran a hand through my short dark hair. Typical response from both of these bureaucrats. Mr. Mayor wanted a piece of my flesh and the council chair wanted to throw money at the problem.

"I appreciate the offer, sir, but by the time we got some new people hired and on the streets, it would be New Year's. I think, though, that we should budget next year for additional part-time assistance, identify some retired law enforcement officers in the area who might want some extra income this time of year."

"Good idea."

I threw a couple more meaningless reassurances at him.

Barnes stood in my office doorway. As usual, her uniform was impeccably clean and pressed, her long, dark hair neatly tucked into a bun. What was unusual was her expression. She was normally a cheerful person, but today, her face was grim.

"I'll keep you posted, Councilman." I disconnected. "Another one?"

"Not yet," she said, with a pessimistic frown. "You going out in the field?"

I pushed myself to a stand. "Yeah, downtown." I retrieved my Glock from my desk and my black wool jacket from the back of my chair.

Barnes had turned to her desk and was pulling her baton out of a drawer. She had it halfway into the loop on her duty belt, when I said, "You can't go."

She whirled around. "Why not?"

"You're overdressed."

CHAPTER TWO

December 21st ~ 9:10 a.m.

Once downtown, I straightened my jacket over the holster at the small of my back, and braced myself to do numbers two and four on my list of four most-hated activities.

Number two was working undercover. I had once loved it, when I was a newly minted Baltimore County detective who still bought into the youthful myth of invincibility. But my enthusiasm had faded fast after losing a partner to friendly fire. During a drug bust that had gone south, a uniform failed to recognize the scruffy-looking buyer as a cop.

Number four was Christmas shopping. I don't believe its presence on the list needs further explanation.

Number one was informing parents that their kid was dead. And number three was driving in snow and ice. One of the many reasons I'd traded in my lieutenant's shield in Maryland for a Chief of Police badge in Starling, Florida.

I fingered that badge in my jacket pocket as I window-shopped along Main Street. The sidewalk was crowded with shoppers, but not as packed as it had been a week ago—when the smash-and-grabs had started.

Christmas tunes wafted from propped open doorways, and more wreaths and green garlands dripped from streetlight posts. White lights, wrapped around the trunks of palm trees, twinkled at me. I grimaced and adjusted my itchy wool jacket, too warm for today's mid-seventies temps.

My Northerner-transplant mind struggled to adapt. Warm breezes in December and Christmas lights on palm trees...it was just *wrong!*

I made note of a leather goods store, to come back to later for a gift for my cousin Paulie. One of the brown vests in the window, maybe. His mother, my aunt and only other living blood relative, was easy. A two-pound box of her favorite chocolates.

I also needed something for Sheriff Sam, my...what? What the hell do you call a quote, "boyfriend," when you're both in your mid-forties? The word *lovers* would get some raised eyebrows, in my city and *especially* in his adjoining rural county. Friends with benefits?

Nah, what we had was more than that, but there was no formal commitment.

He really didn't have any hobbies. Being in charge of an entire sheriff's department, even a small one, tended to eat up most of one's time. What to get him?

And then there was Barnes. Should I give her something? And if so, what?

As if I'd conjured her with my thoughts, she appeared at my elbow, now in civvies. I no longer startle when she materializes out of nowhere like that. Her brother, Bradley—my second in command—contends that she's part witch.

"Nice sweater," I said, eyeing the smiling reindeer face, complete with a red felt ball for a nose.

"Thanks, Ch–"

I scowled at her.

"Sorry, ma'am," she whispered.

We walked along, making small talk—not my forte—just two friends catching up while shopping. She was on the outside, glancing into each shop we passed and then returning her gaze to the crowd in front of us. I was on the inside, turned a little toward her, so I could watch the sidewalk and shops across the street.

It was barely an hour since the last heist, but they had been coming closer together.

A muffled shout from somewhere ahead. A tall, hoodie wearer darted out of a storefront and took off away from us, plowing through the crowd.

Adrenaline spiked. *Hot dog, maybe we're gonna catch this bastard today!*

"Go!" I yelled to Barnes. "I'll check the store."

She was ten feet in front of me, running full out, when a short bald guy ran out of the store and collided with her. She went down.

He didn't, although he stumbled for a few steps. Then he took off again. Light glinted off something in his hand. He was almost as wide as he was tall, but he could run a lot faster than his weight should allow.

"You okay?" I paused beside Barnes.

"Yeah." She was scrambling to her feet.

I bolted after Mr. Baldy, cursing the small-heeled pumps I was wearing. Appropriately professional for the office but not so great for chasing people.

The shopkeeper was yelling at people to get out of his way, but they weren't paying much attention until he was on top of them.

I resisted the urge to call out, "Stop, police!" I didn't want to blow my cover just yet. Hopefully, I could return to being an innocent shopper and try again to catch our perp.

Because I was pretty sure Hoodie Santa was gone. Out in front of the bald guy, there was no more parting of the crowd, and the only pedestrians yelling objections to being shoved aside were those Mr. Baldy was assaulting.

Then a sound that made my blood run cold.

A gunshot.

CHAPTER THREE

December 21st ~ 9:25 a.m.

For a second, the world slowed and went silent. Then people were screaming and bolting in all directions.

I kicked off my shoes and ran harder, wondering briefly where Barnes was.

I reached the bald guy. He had stopped and was huffing and puffing, a silver snub-nose revolver dangling from one hand. I snatched it away from him.

"Hey, that's mine."

"Not anymore." I stuffed it in my pants pocket and grabbed his arm. He tried to pull loose.

Barnes slid to a stop next to us.

I opened my mouth. "Arrest this man–"

A woman's scream interrupted me. "Help! Somebody help this boy."

Barnes grabbed the shopkeeper's other arm, and I took off again.

"Hey," Baldy yelled after me. "You can't arrest me."

I pulled out my badge and held it over my shoulder. I heard scuffling behind me but knew Barnes could handle one short fat guy. The badge slipped out of my hand. I kept going.

The woman screaming for help was older, leaning on a cane. At her feet was a crumpled body. Black jeans and sneakers, dark gray hoodie.

My own gun in my hand now, I said, "Police! Roll over, slowly."

A groan told me the body was alive.

"He's just a boy," the old woman said, scowling at me. "Can't you see he's hurt?"

"Yes, ma'am. Step back, please, so *you* aren't hurt."

She stomped a foot. "Help him!" But she took two steps back.

The body uncurled and flopped over onto its back. Wide dark eyes stared up at me above smooth brown cheeks.

The boy couldn't be a day over fourteen.

One hand clutched his shoulder. The other lay limply at his side.

I crouched and gently patted him down, searching for weapons and also other injuries.

He groaned again. Blood was pooling quickly beneath his shoulder and spreading outward.

I jerked a little when a man stooped beside me. "I was an EMT," he said, in a rich baritone. He was a white guy, with short dark hair and wearing a sleeveless t-shirt and jeans.

I nodded, holstered my gun and shrugged out of my jacket.

He peeled off his t-shirt and wadded it up. Lifting the boy's shoulder, he put the clump of cloth under it, covering the exit wound.

I jammed my jacket against the small entry wound and leaned on it.

"Here," the man said, "I can do that." He gestured with his head to something behind me. "Looks like you're needed elsewhere."

I removed my hands, and he replaced them with the heel of one of his big hands. The boy groaned louder, but the pool of blood had stopped growing.

I rose to my feet and turned.

Barnes stood behind me, one hand hanging onto the handcuffed shopkeeper, the other holding my badge out to me.

Mr. Baldy was spluttering. "Why are you arresting *me*? He's the thief." He pointed his chin toward the boy on the ground.

"What was stolen?" I demanded.

"Jewelry. The case he smashed was full of diamond necklaces and bracelets."

When I'd patted the kid down, I hadn't noticed anything in his pockets that felt like jewelry. I looked down at him. He was no more than my height, five-seven—not the tall guy I'd seen coming out of that store.

Baldy was still spluttering and struggling against Barnes's hold on him.

She wrapped both hands around his upper arm. "Stop it, or we're adding resisting arrest to discharging a firearm in public."

I pulled his pistol out of my pocket. "And assault with a deadly weapon."

"What assault?" Baldy yelled. "I was defending myself."

"You were chasing a man down the street," I said through gritted teeth, "with no good reason to believe he was armed."

"I've got a right to defend my property!"

I took a menacing step toward him. Then winced when my bare foot landed on a sharp rock. It diminished the impact some, but I got in his personal space and glared down at him.

"You shot a firearm into a crowd of innocent people and hit a boy who is *not* the thief!"

"Whadaya mean he's not the thief? He's wearing a hoodie."

I looked around, noting the hoodies near us—half a dozen at least, not counting a pink one on a teenage girl.

But the crowd was getting restless. Things could turn ugly here. Now was not the time to argue with this guy.

Sirens announced an approaching ambulance and backup. One siren stopped nearby. A second later, Sergeant Armstrong's voice was commanding that people step back and make way for the paramedics.

The other siren stopped. The ambulance.

I grabbed Baldy's other arm, and Barnes and I marched him out of the crowd and over to Armstrong's cruiser.

A rookie uniform jumped out of the driver's seat and helped Barnes stuff our prisoner into the backseat.

Then I took a good look at Barnes. Her cheek was scratched, the elbow of her sweater was torn and she was favoring one leg. Blood seeped from the fashionable gap at the knee of her jeans.

"Maybe the paramedics should check you over."

She shook her head vigorously.

I didn't push it. I knew it wouldn't do any good, and in her shoes I wouldn't go to the hospital either.

Speaking of shoes... I looked down at my feet. They were dark with road dust and streaks of clotting blood indicated where they'd encountered multiple rough surfaces.

I raised my head and scanned the crowd. Barnes and I needed to get out of here, go get cleaned up. But first I wanted to thank the good Samaritan with the great baritone voice.

I couldn't spot him in the crowd. Oh well, Armstrong and the other uniforms, who were now taking statements from people, would get his name and contact info. I'd get in touch with him later.

We left the rookie in charge of our prisoner, and Barnes and I limped off to our cars.

CHAPTER FOUR

December 21st ~ 10:15 a.m.

Sergeant Dan Bradley, my second in command, appeared in my office doorway, as I was wolfing down an egg salad sandwich from a nearby deli. A very early lunch, since I hadn't had any breakfast.

"How ya doing, Chief?" His fake grin failed to light up his boyish face. As usual, he was nattily dressed in a navy blazer and khaki slacks.

I swallowed egg and mayonnaise and scowled at him. "I've had better mornings." My feet—cleaned up and sporting several plastic bandages—itched inside my sneakers, which I'd retrieved from my car.

Without prompting, Bradley launched into a report of the latest developments. "Our shop owner, a Mr. Benedict Freeman, has hired a lawyer who is screaming police harassment and false arrest. No coherent or consistent descriptions of the thief. The kid who was shot is at Starling-Shands Hospital. He's an eighth-grader at Bennett Middle School, a solid B student with no record. Stable home, even his parents have never had so much as a parking ticket."

"Anybody find my shoes?" I took another bite of my sandwich.

He shook his head.

I sighed. "What about the bystanders?"

Bradley blinked. "Like I said, not much in the way of consistent descriptions of the guy. Other than the usual dark hoodie and a few glimpses of a Santa mask."

"I meant have you all located the good Samaritan who helped me with the kid?"

Bradley's smooth, thirty-something forehead furrowed. "What good Samaritan?"

I dropped the remnants of my sandwich onto the waxed paper wrapper it had come in. "White guy, brown eyes and hair, wearing jeans, bare-chested. Said he was a former EMT."

Still a blank look from Bradley for a beat. Then he said, "I can go through the uniforms' interview reports again, see if anybody they talked to mentioned helping the kid. What did this guy do?"

"Sacrificed his t-shirt to wad up against the exit wound and put pressure on the wound until the paramedics got there. Then he got swallowed up by the crowd."

"Do you think he has valuable information?"

"Maybe, but at the very least, I'd like to be able to thank him."

"I'll see what I can find out," Bradley said.

"Where are we on known felons with this M.O.?" I asked.

"Twenty-five total in Starling," he reported. "Thirteen currently in prison. Twelve released in the last five years, after serving their time. Uniforms are rounding them up, and we'll interview them."

He sighed. "But...we could be looking at a perp who's moved over to us from Jacksonville. Maybe thinks the pickings are better here."

I nodded, swallowing my own sigh—tracking down all the known robbers in Jacksonville would be a huge task. And this guy might not have a prior record.

Bradley disappeared from my doorway.

He was replaced by Barnes. "Hospital just called. The boy's stable now. He's gonna be okay. They said it was because of your quick action slowing the loss of blood."

"Yeah, well, I didn't do it alone. I wish we could find that guy who helped."

"You could get Derek to do a sketch, with that graphics program he has."

"Good idea." Derek was our resident computer geek. "Get him in here if he's not working on anything crucial."

"What's your definition of crucial?"

"Anything related to catching this smash-and-grab thief. That's first priority, especially now that private citizens are taking it upon themselves to shoot anyone in a hoodie. Who's interviewing the kid?"

"Nobody yet," Barnes said. "He's sedated. The doc said maybe this afternoon. Oh, and by the way, the mayor wants you in his office in half an hour."

I groaned. "You kinda buried the lead there, didn't you, Barnes?"

"Oh, I don't know," she said, with a slight smirk, "who do *you* consider more important, the injured boy or the mayor?"

"I'm not answering that." I stood and grabbed my spare jacket—hanging in the tiny bathroom off of my office. "Tell Derek eleven-thirty, my office. I should be back from my ass-chewing by then."

December 21st ~ 12:15 p.m.

Armstrong, the watch sergeant, was circulating the computer-generated drawing of the good Samaritan to our patrol officers, emphasizing that he was a witness, not a suspect.

In the meantime, I went with the lead detective on the case, Cruthers, to talk to the wounded boy.

Cruthers was a big bear of a man, with shaggy dark hair and a deep, gravelly voice. And yet he had a way with kids.

We entered Justin Cordwell's hospital room, a semi-private with the cloth curtain drawn around the bed closest to the window. I stepped over and peeked around the edge of it. The young man in that bed seemed to be sound asleep. I hoped he stayed that way.

Our boy's mother sat in a chair close to the left side of the bed. Cruthers drew another chair up to the right side and sat, introducing himself as he did so. "And this is Chief Anderson. She was there when you were shot, son, and she wanted to see for herself that you were okay."

"Are you the woman who helped my Justin?" the boy's mama said, half rising from her chair.

I held out my hand. "Yes, ma'am. I'm so–"

She grabbed my hand in both of hers, her eyes shiny. She glanced toward the ceiling. "Thank you, Lord, for sendin' this angel of mercy to save my boy."

I squirmed inside, resisting the urge to pull my hand free. Heat crept up my neck and into my cheeks. I'm not good with mushy stuff.

"I'm glad he's okay," I managed to get out in a relatively normal voice.

Finally, Mrs. Cordwell let go of my hand and settled back into her chair. I took a folded copy of the drawing out of my pocket, unfolded it and showed it to her. "Do you know this man?"

She shook her head.

"Ever seen him before?"

"No, ma'am. Is he the one who shot my boy?"

"No, no," I quickly said. "He also helped slow the bleeding, but I lost track of him in the chaos at the scene, and never got a chance to thank him."

I held the image up for the boy to see. "How about you, Justin, ever seen this guy?"

"No, Mz. Anderson, ma'am."

I gave him a smile. "You can call me Chief. Everybody does."

He nodded. He was a bit ashen, under his medium brown skin tone. White gauze poked up a little above the neckline of his hospital gown, and his left arm was in a sling. But otherwise, he looked okay. I hoped there was no permanent damage to his shoulder muscles.

"Do you happen to know anything about these robberies around town?" I asked him, expecting another negative answer.

But his face brightened, just as his mother popped out of her chair again. "My Justin's a good boy. Never been in trouble in his life."

The boy held up his good hand. "It's okay, Mama. I do know somethin', at least I think it might be somethin'."

We both turned toward him.

"There's a kid at school, says he's a Lit'l Gangsta."

I glanced at Cruthers, my eyebrows in the air, silently asking him who the Lit'l Gangstas were. I stifled a sigh. Maybe someday I'd know this town as well as I'd once known the Baltimore area.

Cruthers shrugged. "Who are the Lit'l Gangstas?" he asked the boy, in a gentle voice.

"I'm not sure. I'd never heard of 'em before. But this kid's been braggin' that his little brothers and sister are gonna have a really good Christmas this year."

"So you're thinking he has something to do with the robberies?" I asked.

The boy nodded. "His name is Tyrone. I can't remember his last name. We aren't friends and he's not in any of my classes. But he's in my grade...eighth."

"Thanks, Justin." I gave one of my cards to his mom, then dug out another one and handed it to him.

He took it and stared at it, seeming a little awestruck.

"You've been a big help. If either of you think of anything else, or hear about anything, give me a call."

Once we were down the hall a bit, Cruthers said, "Tyrone, eighth grade, Bennett Middle School. He shouldn't be that hard to track down."

"Hope you don't mind me giving them my card, instead of yours."

"Nah, you seemed to have a rapport with them. My motto is always go with what works... Can I drop you off at 3MB?" he added. "I wanna roust my CI and see if he knows anything about these Lit'l Gangstas. And having the police chief along might freak him out."

"No problem." The presence of the Chief of Police might indeed make a confidential informant quite nervous.

Outside, we walked toward his car. "Where's Barnes?" he asked.

"She took a couple hours off to finish her Christmas shopping."

He grimaced.

"I take it you haven't finished yours," I said.

"I haven't even started. How about you?"

"I've given it some thought."

He let out a low rumble of a chuckle.

CHAPTER FIVE

December 21st ~ 12:55 p.m.

Back at the department, I strode across the bullpen toward my office.

Bradley popped out of his office door and fell into step with me. "We got lucky, I think."

I lifted an eyebrow at him but kept walking.

"The crime scene guys were able to lift partials of several bloody fingerprints, from the sidewalk around where the kid went down. Most of them were the responding paramedics. But one wasn't. Shall I run it to see if it nets us your good Samaritan?"

I gave a half shrug. "This guy seemed like an upstanding citizen, but yeah, see if he's in the system."

Bradley nodded. "Oh, and the trigger-happy shop owner is worried about getting his gun back."

I snorted. "When donkeys fly!"

He gave me one of his half smiles, one end of his mouth quirking up. "I told his lawyer it was evidence, and he may or may not get it back after the case is resolved."

"Have you ever heard of the Lit'l Gangstas?" I asked, as we reached my office. "They might be a gang."

Bradley shook his head and followed me in, stopping just inside the door. "To the best of my knowledge, there's no gang in Starling by that name... Where's my sis?"

"She took the rest of the afternoon off to do some Christmas shopping."

He cocked an eyebrow in the air—Bradley has very expressive eyebrows. "Really? She's usually a last-minute shopper, or she gives gift cards."

I shook my head slightly. "Do all cops hate Christmas shopping?"

"Not me," he said. "All my gifts are bought and wrapped already."

I gave him a mock glare. "Get out of here, Mr. Goody-Two-Shoes."

He chuckled as he turned and left my office.

⚬⚬⚬

December 21st ~ 1:20 p.m.

Less than a half hour later, Bradley was back, a printed-out mug shot in his hand. "That partial fingerprint seems to belong to this guy." He handed it over.

The man in the picture looked a lot rougher than the one who'd helped me with Justin. His hair was shoulder length and unkempt, his beard scraggly, and his eyes bloodshot.

But it was the good Samaritan. His name was Jacob Woods, and he'd served three and a half years of a six-year sentence for burglary of a doctor's office and possession of drugs.

Hmm, seems he cleaned up his act when he got out of prison...or maybe in prison.

"He was an EMT," Bradley added, "until a back injury on the job. Then he got hooked on opioids and it all went downhill from there. Oh, and he has a sealed juvenile record."

I handed the mug shot back. "I think it's better to keep using my sketch. It's closer to how he looks now. Add his name to the BOLO though, again with the reminder that he's a witness, not a suspect. And–"

"Track down his parole officer," Bradley said. "On it."

December 21st ~ 1:45 p.m.

I was considering ducking out and doing some Christmas shopping of my own—maybe go back to that leather goods store—when Cruthers strolled into the bullpen.

He meandered over to my open office door and stuck his head in. "I've got Tyrone Williams cooling his heels in a holding cell. His mama's on her way in. Wanna sit in on the interrogation?"

"What'd you arrest him for?"

"Fool kid took a swing at me, when I said I needed him to come in for a chat."

I pushed myself to a stand. "You take it, and I'll observe."

I made myself comfortable in the small observation area next to the largest of our two interrogation rooms. Space was tight in 3MB. I hoped, in another year or so, that I'd be able to convince the city's powers-that-be to let us expand.

My daydreams of our own spacious building, not under the direct eye of Mr. Mayor and the city council, were interrupted when Cruthers brought the kid into the room next door. He was white, dark-haired, and again about my height.

His mother trailed behind, looking more anxious than the kid did. I switched on the video and audio recorders.

But the interview was a bust. All the kid would say, besides "I wanna damn lawyer," was "I hate the poe-lice."

Awfully young to have such an attitude already.

His mother admonished him, and he fell into a sullen silence.

"I'll get you your lawyer, son," Cruthers said, as he re-cuffed him. "But here's something to think about while you're waiting for him. Assaulting a police officer can be either a misdemeanor or a felony. Some cooperation from you, and you get a slap on the wrist. No cooperation and you're looking at a year, or more, in juvie hall."

His mother paled, but the kid defiantly stuck his chin out.

A few minutes later, we were back in my office, Cruthers ensconced in the one comfortable visitor's chair. I had two others—chrome and vinyl contraptions I'd inherited from the previous chief. They had visitors squirming to leave within a minute of sitting down. My people knew they'd screwed up if I directed them to one of those chairs.

"The kid's got a record," Cruthers said. "But nothing major. Several shoplifting charges, and he went joyriding with some older friends one time, in a stolen car. They got grand theft auto, but he was only charged with unauthorized use of a vehicle."

"So why did he take a swing at you?" I asked.

Cruthers shrugged. "He seemed to be cooperative, until I mentioned the Lit'l Gangstas. That's when he pulled loose from me and cranked back his fist. I ducked and had him cuffed before he knew what hit him."

"Not much of a street fighter, then."

"Nope."

Bradley appeared in my doorway. "Hey, Cruthers..."

The older detective nodded but made no move to get up. Bradley gave him a mock scowl.

"Age before beauty," Cruthers said with a grin.

I hid my own smile. He'd used that line before to stake his claim on the comfy chair, over that of his younger supervisor.

Bradley's mouth quirked up on one end. He remained standing. "So far, we've got five viable suspects, Chief, from the list of guys with robbery priors. The uniforms are still looking for the others."

"Any luck tracking down Mr. Woods?" I asked.

Bradley shook his head. "Got a call in to his parole officer."

Cruthers opened his mouth. "I think–"

But we never found out what Cruthers thought. The sounds of a noisy scuffle interrupted him.

Bradley turned in the doorway, then took off across the bullpen. Cruthers and I jumped up and ran out of my office.

We halted at the sight of Barnes dragging a short, squat Santa Claus toward us. Her sweater was stretched out of shape, hanging off of one shoulder, and Rudolph's felt nose was dangling by a few threads. The tear in the knee of her jeans was now way too big to be fashionable.

But she was grinning.

Her prisoner was pulling back, trying to jerk loose from her double-handed hold on his upper arm. "Hey, you all cops?" he yelled at us. "Arrest this crazy bitch. Ain't no law against dressin' up like Santa."

One of her hands let go of his bicep and reached into the pocket of his oversized jeans.

He tried to jerk away again. "Hey lady, stop feelin' me up."

"Not arresting you for dressing like Santa," she said, huffing a little. Her hand came out of the pocket and held up a fistful of brightly wrapped candies. "But it is illegal to rob a candy store."

CHAPTER SIX

December 21st ~ 2:35 p.m.

Sweet-tooth Santa was African-American, about five-six, and built like a miniature linebacker. His name was Dominic Johnson, and his record was clean other than two shoplifting charges. He seemed willing to talk, and I planned to let Barnes take a crack at interrogating him. It was her collar, after all. But I'd insisted we wait for his mother to arrive. His school ID said he was only thirteen.

Then the call came in, another smash-and-grab at a high-end gift shop, just forty minutes after the candy store had been hit. And the gift shop was on the opposite side of town from the candy store.

Damn! The pattern was starting to make sense.

Ten minutes later, Dominic's mom had arrived and everything was good to go in the main interrogation room. The boy had been Mirandized, the mother seated beside him, and the recording equipment was activated. I watched the video in the observation room next door.

I was somewhat concerned that Barnes would be too gung-ho with this first interrogation. But I'd underestimated her.

"Dominic," she began in a gentle voice, "your mom says you're a good kid."

The mother nodded vigorously, but her light brown skin had turned a bit gray.

"And I looked up your record," Barnes continued, "only a couple of shoplifting charges." She leaned back in her chair, her confident but casual demeanor almost making up for the forlorn-looking reindeer on her now over-sized sweater. "I'm thinkin' that you really don't want to spend Christmas in jail."

The mother's mouth fell open, but she didn't say anything.

"So here's what we want to know," Barnes said, her tone still casual. "Who put you up to robbing that candy store?"

The boy shook his head slightly.

"Was it the Lit'l Gangstas?" Barnes asked.

The boy's eyes went wide. He glanced at his mother and shook his head more vigorously.

I think he doth protest too much.

"What you doin' hangin' out with them?" his mother demanded.

"Do you know anything about them, ma'am?" Barnes asked.

"No, but anything with Gangsta in it, that can't be good." Her expression tense, eyes full of worry, she turned back to her son. "You tell this lady whatever you know, right now."

Don't correct her, I thought, willing Barnes to let the *this lady* go. Even though it should be *this officer.*

I needn't have worried. Barnes was silent, waiting.

The kid was shaking his head again, but hesitantly this time. His gaze remained on his mother's face. I suspected he was more afraid of her wrath than anything the law could do to him.

"I don't know nothin'," he claimed. But he was quaking in his baggy clothes.

Barnes leaned forward a little. "Look, Dominic, this could go three ways. You could be charged with a felony for robbery. It could be a third-degree felony for a smash and grab. That's five years in prison. Or a second-degree felony for robbery. That's up to fifteen years."

I was impressed. Barnes had done her homework. Although the charges and sentences she'd quoted were for adults. This kid would be going to a juvie facility, and for no more than five years, when he'd be eighteen. But I had no problem with her throwing the fear of a long prison sentence into him, if it got him talking.

"That's a really long time to be locked up for some handfuls of candy." She leaned farther forward. "*Or* we can ask the State's Attorney's office to file it as another shoplifting charge, a misdemeanor. That could be as little as thirty days." She paused. "Or maybe no jail time at all, just community service, if you cooperate."

She paused again, let all that sink in.

Dominic's gaze was fixed on Rudolph's dangling nose. He now looked ready to puke.

His mom's lips were set in a firm line. "Boy, you better start talkin' *now*."

"I don't know nothin' about any other Lit'l Gangstas." His words now poured out. "It's not really a gang. There's this guy, a white dude, he gave us the Santa masks..." He trailed off, glanced at his mother's face and back to Barnes again.

He swallowed hard. "He's trying to get some poor kids a better Christmas. He fences the stuff and uses it to buy toys." The kid sat up straighter in his chair. "We're all gonna help him take them around to folks' houses on Christmas Eve."

Barnes's eyebrows were both in the air, but otherwise she was controlling her facial expression. "He's gonna fence candy?"

The kid shook his head. "No, the Lit'l Gangstas, we hit one store, and then he hits another himself. It's, you know, like a..."

"Diversion," his mother supplied.

"We get to keep what we take," her son continued, "for us and our own families."

I was nodding inside the observation room. That's what I'd begun to suspect.

Barnes asked the kid for a description of the white guy, but I didn't wait to hear his answer. I power-walked back to the bullpen.

"Bradley," I called out as soon as I stepped inside it.

He popped out of his office. "What's up, Chief?"

"Have the watch sergeant call in the auxiliary folks. Let them cover routine stuff. I want every sworn officer—including the ones who are off-duty—in plain clothes, covering the jewelry shops, high-end boutiques, and electronics stores around town. Next time a cheaper place is hit, no flocking of officers to that call. Instead, they head for the opposite side of the city and backup the cops already there."

I paused, sucked in air. "We are gonna catch this bastard!"

———◦———

December 21st ~ 3:25 p.m.

Bradley lounged in my comfy visitor's chair. He'd just reported that the five ex-cons they'd rounded up so far, with similar smash-and-grab MOs, had all been interviewed. "Three have alibis for most of the robberies. They were working and their coworkers or bosses vouched for them. That leaves two viable suspects, although they're both denying it, of course. I sent their records and mug shots to you." He poked a thumb in the direction of my computer monitor.

"Ricardo Diaz," he said, as I leaned forward and clicked on the appropriate mug shot. "Cuban-American. Did four years for armed robbery."

"Wouldn't smash-and-grabs be coming down a notch or two for him?" I asked. The face in front of me was broad, the expression vacant, his skin tone light beige. "Dominic could've mistaken him for white."

"He had a handgun on him when he was arrested, caught in the act. Thus the upgrade to armed robbery, but his MO was smash-and-grab. He hit mainly pawn shops."

"What's that tattoo on his neck?"

"Gang tats. It's not a gang that operates in Starling, but they are in Raiford prison. He probably joined there."

"Eat or be eaten," I commented.

Bradley snorted. "As in, join or be shanked."

I nodded grimly, then moved over to the other mug shot, a heavy-jowled, white thirty-something. "This guy looks vaguely familiar."

"Clarence 'Junior' Phillips," he said. "He's done two stints for robbing convenience stores."

"I wonder if he's any relation to a detective we had in Baltimore County years ago." I sat back in my desk chair. "Laziest s.o.b. ever. Got canned for royally botching a case. As a matter of fact, that was the case where I first met Kate Huntington."

"The psychologist you sometimes consult with... She worked on that one?"

I shook my head. "No, she was the suspect. Her first husband was killed, and this Phillips clown tried to pin it on her and a lawyer friend, assumed they were lovers. He didn't even look for other leads. She and her friends tracked down the real killer themselves."

My chest grew warm at the thought of Kate and her little band of loyal friends and family. Even the memory of her second husband, a private investigator who'd been a pain in my backside more than once, didn't annoy me anymore.

"Well, Junior here," Bradley was saying, poking his thumb toward my monitor again, "he isn't the brightest bulb, that's for sure. He doesn't have an alibi for any of our robberies, and his parole officer says he's missed two check-ins. He was about to rescind his parole anyway."

He paused. "And speaking of parole officers, I got ahold of the one who has your good Samaritan's case. He said Woods has been squeaky clean ever since he got out of prison nine months ago. He sells used cars. Shows up for all his appointments on time, yada, yada. Goes to Narcotics Anonymous meetings regularly as well."

"You sound skeptical."

He shrugged.

"Some convicts do go straight after they get out," I observed.

He shrugged again. "He seems to be one of them. I sent a uniform to his job to politely ask him to come in when he has a moment, so you can thank him."

"Good, thanks. What about our gun-happy shop owner?"

Bradley gave me that half-smile of his. "He was arraigned a couple of hours ago. The judge shared your dismay that he'd shot an unarmed, innocent bystander, a kid, no less. Bail was set at $100,000. He squawked that he couldn't afford the ten percent bail-bondsman's fee, so he will be a guest of the city for now."

I didn't bother to hide my smirk.

But it was wiped off my face when Barnes entered my office, carrying the local newspaper. She held it up, showing us the headline of the top story.

Shop Owner Arrested; Robberies Continue.

As headlines go, it could've been worse. But the article below it was a different story. The reporter implied the police were derelict at best, stupid at worst, for arresting an otherwise law-abiding citizen who was trying to protect his property.

"Sheez, Louise," I exclaimed, "that kid could've died."

"And if he had, the paper would've been appropriately outraged," Bradley said, with a hint of sarcasm. "And they'd be blasting us for not stopping it from happening."

I grimaced. These days, cops were between a rock and a hard place most of the time.

"Barnes," I asked, "did you get anything else interesting out of Dominic Johnson?"

"His description of this *Robin* Hoodie Santa is pretty generic." She chuckled at her own joke.

I frowned at her.

She cleared her throat. "Slightly above average height, average build. Medium brown hair. Wore a hoodie and jeans. Kid can't remember his eye color. Should I have him work with Derek to come up with a sketch?"

I shook my head. "First, we'll put together a lineup, with Phillips and Diaz in it. Let's see if we can speed things up by getting Dominic to identify *Robin Hoodie*."

CHAPTER SEVEN

December 21st ~ 4:30 p.m.

The lineup had been a bust. Dominic didn't recognize either of the men. I wasn't particularly surprised. Phillips didn't seem smart enough to have organized this whole operation. And Diaz's thousand-yard stare and gang tats didn't fit with him collecting toys for poor kids. Unless...

Maybe he was scamming the kids and planned to keep it all for himself. *That seems more likely*, my cynical cop brain thought.

But Dominic hadn't identified him. Or maybe he'd lied.

Diaz was pretty scary looking. Could be the kid was afraid to finger him.

Bradley and Cruthers were interrogating both men again, to see if they could shake anything loose. And uniforms were still tracking down the other ex-cons with similar MOs.

Of course, it was possible our perp didn't have an arrest history. I doubted that, though. One didn't get this good, this organized, without practice.

Or maybe he was good at it all along, or just damned lucky, and had never been caught.

Barnes came into my office and sank onto the comfy chair. "Now what do we do, wait for this guy to strike again?" Her expression was forlorn. "What if he decides we're getting too close and he stops?"

I grimaced. "Not sure how I'd feel about that. No more robberies would be good, but..."

"We'll still look like we're incompetent," she finished my sentence. "And people will still be scared to shop here in Starling, 'cause they won't know for sure it's safe."

"*And*," I added, "this bastard will have gotten away with it."

I sighed. Time to adjust my expectations. We might not catch this s.o.b. before Christmas.

That thought gave me another idea. "Get together a list of the poorest neighborhoods in the city. If we don't catch him before then, we'll get our Robin Hoodie Santa when he tries to distribute his bounty on Christmas Eve."

She nodded and left my office.

And I turned back to the day's incident reports, scrolling through them as quickly as possible. I tried to look at all of them, to stay on top of what was going on in my department and my city. But the number of reports were three times the norm this close to Christmas. Shoplifters and pickpockets were upping their game. And as the stress of the holiday prep got to people, bar fights and domestic violence calls went up as well. As did the drunk-and-disorderlies.

The auxiliary group was handling whatever they could. I avoid calling them auxiliary police—they aren't sworn officers, and their training is minimal. Some of my people are openly scornful of the "wannabe cops," but right now I wasn't sure what I'd do without them.

I had two open billets for new uniformed officers and an opening for a detective. I seemed to be losing people as fast as I hired new ones. A couple of them had gone to jail, as the rampant corruption during the previous police chief's watch had come to light.

My administrative worries were interrupted when Bradley's head came around the frame of my open doorway.

"We might have some good suspects this time. Two brothers from our ex-con list, James and John Hitchcock." He pointed at my computer.

I opened my email and clicked on the images attached to his message.

"They've been out about three months," Bradley was saying, "after a two-year stint for robbery. Neither showed up for work today and their mother, with whom they're living, hasn't seen them in a while."

I perused the mug shots. They were white, the right height and build, and their sandy hair could easily be died darker.

"They hit a dozen stores three years ago," he continued, "here and in Jacksonville. One would distract the clerks while the other would pocket as much merchandise as possible."

"So why are they recruiting kids as their distractions now?"

"Good question. A uniform is sitting on Mom's house, in case they come home."

"Chief," Barnes's voice from behind her brother. "Call just came in. Toy store on the east side."

"Or," Bradley said with a grin, "we might catch them in the act."

December 21st ~ 4:45 p.m.

Hot damn! I jumped up, grabbed my jacket off the back of my chair. My Glock came out of the desk drawer and slipped smoothly into the holster at the back of my waistband.

"Any guesses as to the most likely target?" I shrugged into my jacket as the three of us jogged across the bullpen.

"Yeah," Bradley said, "there are two high-end jewelry stores that haven't been hit yet, on the west side of town."

I nodded.

Barnes, a little ahead of us, stopped at the elevators.

"Come on," I said. "Fire stairs are faster." I was anxious to be in on the take-down of this thief who'd been making us look like fools.

We took the unmarked sedan that Bradley drove when on duty. In Maryland, it would be dusk already, quickly moving toward full dark. But the Florida sun still hung in the sky, a bright yellow ball just above the western skyline.

We entered the ritzy westside shopping district. The sidewalks were fake cobblestone, aiming for quaint, even though this area of town hadn't been developed until the 1990s. More Christmas lights winked at us from poles and palm trees. A large decorated pine rose from the center of a round-about.

"No parking left on the street," Bradley said.

"Go in that paid lot," I said. "I see some spaces." I glanced over my shoulder. "Barnes, you stroll along the sidewalk, like you're on foot patrol, in front of one of the two jewelry stores. Bradley, you and I will take the other. We're siblings shopping for a present for our very picky mother."

Ten minutes later, we were staring down into a glass display case. A clerk—raising his voice slightly to be heard over the obligatory Christmas music piped throughout the store—was extolling the virtues of various diamond necklaces.

And I was trying not to gasp at their prices. "Are those last two zeroes *after* the decimal point?"

The clerk sniffed. "No, ma'am."

I pursed my lips, trying to look unimpressed. The necklace in question cost twice my yearly income.

"Don't worry, Sis," Bradley said. "I know you can't afford half on a teacher's salary. I'll cover most of it."

I gave him a sisterly glare. But I had to admit he looked the part of a successful businessman. He was a clotheshorse, by far the best dressed member of the department.

"Can we see some with a few less zeroes in the price?" he asked the clerk.

Another sniff from the clerk. "Maybe a nice bracelet?"

"Yeah, that's a good idea," Bradley said.

Movement in the corner of my eye. I twisted my head toward the plate glass window.

A guy in a Santa mask and hoodie was running by.

"Come on!" I yelled and bolted for the door.

CHAPTER EIGHT

December 21ˢᵗ ~ 5:16 p.m.

My sneakers hadn't really gone well with the buying-an-expensive-gift-for-our-mother ruse, but I was damned glad to have them on my feet now.

Barnes whizzed past us as we exited the store. We both took off after her.

Bradley, a decade younger than me, pulled out in front. "Stop! Police!" he huffed out.

A guilty flash of petty satisfaction that his running faster was costing him.

Half a block later, Barnes tackled the thief. Bradley—right behind them—couldn't stop in time. They all went down in a heap.

Bradley rolled off, but held onto one of the guy's arms. Barnes half stood, and was cuffing the perp when I caught up. She rolled him over.

I reached down and snatched the Santa mask off his face...and gasped.

Neither the Hitchcock brothers nor Ricardo Diaz were staring up at me. Our Robin Hoodie Santa was Jacob Woods, my good Samaritan!

December 21st ~ 6:05 p.m.

I'd pulled rank and was interrogating Woods myself. He'd been Mirandized and had declined a lawyer.

"For now," he'd said in that rich baritone, as he sat across the interrogation room's table from me. His black hoodie was unzipped, revealing a white t-shirt, stretched taut over his muscled chest. His dark eyes locked on mine, showing interest but no anxiety.

I cut to the chase. "We've caught you in the act, so why not confess?"

"I might be inclined to do that." His quick reply surprised me.

"If you agree to my terms," he added.

I bristled. "I'm usually the one who's setting the *terms* of a deal."

He said nothing.

"This morning, when we were helping the kid who'd been shot, you'd ditched your hoodie somewhere, hadn't you? Along with the Santa mask. Then you circled back."

"I might be willing to discuss that." He cleared his throat. "If you'll do me a *favor*... Maybe you prefer that wording."

After a beat, I said, "Go on. What's the favor?"

"Let's say, hypothetically, that most of what was taken has been converted into cash and used to purchase toys. There are some *alleged* stolen goods, in a rented warehouse—things that I, *hypothetically*, haven't had a chance to fence yet. But mostly it's full of new toys."

Woods leaned forward across the table. "But now they are *used* toys, not really worth much in terms of cash value."

I had a feeling where this was going and wasn't at all sure how I'd respond.

"Sooo," he dragged out the word, "no point in selling them to make reparations to the store owners. They'd only get maybe five cents on the dollar." He paused. "If you will promise to distribute those toys to the kids who won't otherwise have a Christmas, I will give you my confession."

"And I suppose that you'll want to play Santa." My tone was acerbic. "And give out the toys yourself."

He shook his head. "You can take the credit, or the store owners can say they donated the toys. I don't care how you spin it, as long as the toys make it to the kids."

"I'll have to run it past the store owners first."

He nodded.

"Another question." My tone remained crisp. Why was I so pissed at this guy?

"Go ahead."

"Why'd you do it?"

He stared at me for a moment, then blew out a sigh. "I grew up poor. Christmas meant we got a decent meal, turkey and the fixings at the local soup kitchen. And pumpkin pie. Don't get me wrong, I was grateful for a full belly for a change. But I couldn't figure out why Santa never brought me anything. Even though I tried really hard to be good all year..."

He paused, his Adam's apple bobbing in his throat as he swallowed. "I figured I must be an intrinsically bad kid, no matter how hard I tried. So I *became* a bad kid."

My chest had begun to ache. Hanging onto my sarcasm as a shield, I said, "And where did a bad kid learn the word *intrinsically*?"

He gave me a cheeky grin. "The tiny library at juvie hall. I got myself straightened out eventually, got my GED, took the EMT training. Life was good for a while, until I hurt my back." He shifted in his chair and winced.

Should I believe the wince or was that an act? I shook my head slightly, staring at the man. *What a waste.*

Out loud, I said, "And now you're going back to prison."

"It's not all bad. Last time, I got my AA degree. This time I'm going for my bachelor's, on the state's dime."

"Ya know, there are easier ways to work your way through school."

He grinned again and shrugged his broad shoulders.

Then his face sobered. "Look, I was only trying to give some kids a sense of self-worth. That they deserved some toys from Santa, just like any other kid. It's enough of an uphill battle for them to have a decent life when they're grown. They need to believe in themselves, that they're worth it."

I frowned, the ache in my chest a bit stronger. I turned the frown into a full-blown scowl, to cover my feelings. "You're facing charges for contributing to the delinquency of minors as well. You enticed those kids to commit robbery."

He actually hung his head some. "I only recruited ones that were already headed down that path. Figured I'd put them to work for a good cause. And they were only shoplifting."

"Which *is* a crime."

He nodded, looked away.

"Why didn't you stop, after that kid got shot?"

"I wanted to." He glanced back toward me, without making eye contact. "I have a list of kids, whose parents can't afford enough food for them, much less gifts. We only needed a little more money..." He trailed off, then finally looked me in the eye. "I told the boys I'd recruited that it would be okay if they didn't want to help anymore. Most of them did, though."

I shoved myself to a stand. "I'll talk to the store owners."

He nodded again, a slight grin returning to his face. "I'm not going anywhere."

EPILOGUE

December 24th ~ 2:00 p.m.

The store owners had balked at first. But our department's Public Information Officer, Phyllis Gladstone convinced them. She'd advertised the *Christmas Extravaganza for Deserving Kids* in the local paper, and had listed all the stores as sponsors.

The stolen goods that hadn't yet been fenced were now in our evidence room, and they would eventually be returned to their rightful owners. Those shopkeepers had gratefully donated some funds to help with the shortfall. And Phyl had taken up a collection throughout the municipal building. Between those two sources, there was more than enough to purchase the rest of the toys needed.

The giveaway was staged in the warehouse Jacob Woods had rented—his lease was paid up through the thirty-first. The auxiliary folks had pitched in to get the place decorated and the toys stuffed into gift bags. Garlands swathed cement-block walls and tinsel hung from the rafters. A big Christmas tree had been donated by the mayor's office—of course, he'd had to get in on the act.

I admitted to myself that it did look festive. Kind of uplifting.

Several bakeries had donated refreshments. Kids and parents arrived by the busload.

A straight-backed chair, draped in red velvet, sat in the middle of the floor. Cruthers perched on it, in a Santa suit augmented by a pillow to give him a rounder belly. His dark hair was temporarily whitened with baby powder, and his red hat perched at a rakish angle. He grinned through his fake beard, as he passed out the gift bags.

Halfway through the festivities, Barnes leaned over next to my ear. "Maybe the police department should sponsor this every year. Get the merchants to donate the toys, and such."

I turned to her. "That's an excellent idea."

I paused for effect, watching her smile spread, then I added, "You're in charge of organizing it."

Her face fell. But she quickly rallied. "You got it, Chief."

~~*

AUTHOR'S NOTES

I hope you enjoyed this Christmas story and will check out the other books in the C.o.P. on the Scene Mysteries, starring Chief of Police Judith Anderson and her Starling, Florida police department—*Lethal Assumptions* and *Fatal Escape*.

Book 4, *Felony Murder*, will hopefully be released in late 2023 (see below for an excerpt).

I totally enjoyed writing this novelette. I love holiday-themed stories, and a new series gave me the perfect excuse to write one. And I couldn't resist giving Officer Barnes an "ugly" Christmas sweater.

I am very grateful to my sister authors at *misterio press* who helped me polish this story, and to my husband who did the final proofread.

We pride ourselves at *misterio* on producing books with as few errors as possible, but proofreaders are human (including Hubs). If you noticed any typos, please email and let me know so we can get them corrected. My email is kass@kass andralamb.com.

Indeed, email me anyway I'm always thrilled to hear from readers!

Excerpt from *Felony Murder*:

CHAPTER ONE

My private line rang, interrupting my train of thought.

I grabbed the receiver and barked a hello into it, realizing too late that my annoyed tone wasn't a good thing. Only a few key people had my private number—like the mayor and the city council chair.

Silence on the line.

Yup, I'd pissed somebody off.

Not the first time, I thought, *won't be the last.*

"Chief Anderson?" A tentative voice, male...and young.

"Yes." I tried for neutral but the tone was still a bit brusque.

"I'm sorry to bother you, ma'am, but I've run out of options. My trial is coming up in two weeks and I'm innocent. But I could end up in the electric ch–"

"Who the hell is this?" I yelled into the phone. "And how did you get this number?"

My assistant, Officer Gloria Barnes, appeared in my office doorway. As usual, her uniform was impeccable, but her forehead was creased, her lips a thin line.

A beat of silence, then the man said, "If I answer the second question, will you hear me out?"

I ground my teeth but forced myself to stop and think. Yes, finding out how he'd gotten my number merited a few minutes of my time. "You've got two minutes."

"My name is Juan Alvarez."

He had no accent, so not a first-generation immigrant. In Florida, he was most likely Cuban-American.

"I'm going to trial soon on a felony murder charge," he said, his voice frantic. "A drug deal gone wrong. But I wasn't there. I had nothing to do with it."

"What's the case number?"

I was surprised when he rattled it off. I had to ask him to repeat it so I could write it down.

Most accused who were awaiting trial had no idea what their case number was. They weren't bright enough to realize it was a useful piece of information when dealing with law enforcement and/or the legal system.

I no longer thought of it as the justice system, because justice did not always prevail. Instead, it enforced the law—most of the time—for better or worse.

"Will you look into my case? I tell you, I'm being set up."

"I'll take a look at the file." I stopped, took a deep breath. "Beyond that, no promises. But only if you tell me how you got my private line number."

"It's on the bathroom wall on the men's side of the jail."

A voice, half yelling in the background.

"Gotta go." Juan disconnected.

I cussed a blue streak.

Barnes stepped into my office. "Chief?"

"Get the number changed for my private line."

I shook my head slightly as I looked over the case file.

Juan Flores Alvarez was indeed about to go to trial for felony murder, during a drug deal that had apparently gone terribly wrong. The dead man was one Miguel Acosta

Juarez. Alvarez's two compadres had both cut deals to lower their sentences, fingering Alvarez.

But no one had admitted to pulling the trigger of the gun that had actually killed Juarez. And there had been no gunpowder residue on Juan Alvarez's hands.

I sat back in my chair and sighed.

My private line rang. My heart rate jacked up a notch. Then I glanced at the caller ID and breathed out another sigh, this one relieved. I knew this number. "Hello."

"Hey there." Sheriff Sam's lovely baritone.

"How's your day going?" he asked.

I took a deep breath, trying to decide if I should pretend everything was hunky-dory or 'fess up that I was having a lousy morning.

"That bad, huh?" There was no fooling Sam. He knew me too well.

"Some guy with a felony murder charge hanging over his head got a hold of my private line number."

A beat of silence. "Not good." His voice was grim.

"It gets worse. He got it off the men's room wall in the jail."

Sam's turn to cuss a blue streak. The jail was under his purview as the Clover County sheriff.

~~

ABOUT THE AUTHOR

Kassandra Lamb has never been able to decide which she loves more, psychology or writing. In college, she realized that writers need a day job in order to eat, so she studied psychology. After a career as a psychotherapist and college professor, she is now retired and can pursue her passion for writing.

She spends most of her time in an alternate universe with her characters. The portal to that universe, aka her computer, is located in Florida, where her husband and dog catch occasional glimpses of her.

Kass has completed the ten-book, traditional mystery series, The Kate Huntington Mysteries (set in her native Maryland, about a psychotherapist/amateur sleuth), plus four Kate on Vacation novellas (with the same main characters). She is also the author of the thirteen-book Marcia Banks and Buddy cozy mystery series, about a service dog trainer and her sidekick and mentor dog, Buddy, set in north central Florida.

And she has started a new series of police procedurals, with Lieutenant Judith Anderson from the Kate Huntington series as the main character in the C.o.P. on the Scene Mysteries (three stories out with more to come).

To read and see more about Kassandra and her books, please go to https://kassandralamb.com. Be sure to sign up for the newsletter there to get a heads up about new releases, plus special offers and bonuses for subscribers (and free stories).

Kass's e-mail is kass@kassandralamb.com and she loves hearing from readers! She's also on Facebook and Goodreads and she blogs about psychological topics and other random things at https://misteriopress.com.

Kassandra also writes romantic suspense under the pen name of Jessica Dale.

~~

Other misterio press Series

Karma's A Bitch: Pet Psychic Mysteries
by Shannon Esposito

Multiple Motives: Kate Huntington Mysteries
by Kassandra Lamb

The Metaphysical Detective: Riga Hayworth Paranormal
Mysteries
by Kirsten Weiss

Dangerous and Unseemly: Concordia Wells Historical
Mysteries
by K.B. Owen

Murder, Honey: Carol Sabala Mysteries
by Vinnie Hansen

Payback: Unintended Consequences Romantic Suspense
by Jessica Dale

Full Mortality: Nikki Latrelle Mysteries
by Sasscer Hill

<u>Buried in the Dark: Frankie O'Farrell Mysteries</u>
by Shannon Esposito

<u>To Kill A Labrador: Marcia Banks and Buddy Cozy
Mysteries</u>
by Kassandra Lamb

<u>Never Sleep: Chronicles of a Lady Detective Historical
Mysteries</u>
by K.B. Owen

<u>Bound: Witches of Doyle Cozy Mysteries</u>
by Kirsten Weiss

<u>At Wits' End Cozy Mysteries</u>
by Kirsten Weiss

<u>Steeped In Murder: Tea and Tarot Mysteries</u>
by Kirsten Weiss

<u>The Perfectly Proper Paranormal Museum Mysteries</u>
by Kirsten Weiss

<u>Big Shot: The Big Murder Mysteries</u>
by Kirsten Weiss

<u>Steam and Sensibility: Sensibility Grey Steampunk
Mysteries</u>
by Kirsten Weiss

<u>Maui Widow Waltz: Islands of Aloha Mysteries</u>
by JoAnn Bassett

Plus even more great mysteries/thrillers in the *misterio press* bookstore.

www.ingramcontent.com/pod-product-compliance
Lightning Source LLC
Chambersburg PA
CBHW020649130626
46552CB00003B/1468